Where the Mind Finds Its Escape

Ctrl+Alt = Desire

Darron Thomas

Ctrl+Alt=Desire: Where the Mind Finds Its Escape
© 2025 by Darron Thomas

ISBNs:
Hardback: 979-8-9930422-0-6
Paperback: 979-8-9930422-1-3
Ebook (EPUB): 979-8-9930422-2-0
Downloadable audio file: 979-8-9930422-3-7
Digital online: 979-8-9930422-4-4

Cover design by 100 Covers
Copyedited by Rachel Keith
Narrated by Sharman Wilkinson

First Edition: 2026

For the women who raised me, taught me, and shaped me.

Growing up in a home filled with four generations of women—my sister, my mother, my grandmother, and my great-grandmother—I learned the power of observation, of listening, and of truly understanding. Their wisdom, their love, and even their struggles gave me the lens through which I see the world today.

This book is dedicated first to them, and then to every woman—past, present, and future—whose voice, presence, and truth deserve to be seen and heard.

"We live our lives in order,
yet our minds wander to places
we're told never to go."

TABLE OF CONTENTS

CHAPTER 1

Chloe

T he GPS on Chloe's phone droned its monotonous directions, each familiar turn a nail in the coffin of her post-college expectations. Her life these days, a sterile landscape of spreadsheets, was a far cry from the vibrant future she'd imagined, and tonight the emptiness felt particularly heavy. The hollowness churning in her gut mirrored the restless current that had buzzed beneath the surface all day.

Usually she'd succumb to the routine: highway home, frozen dinner, the anesthetizing scroll of Instagram. But tonight the thrum was louder, a restless energy demanding release. As her usual exit approached, Chloe made a sudden, impulsive turn onto a winding road she'd only ever glanced at.

"Recalculating . . ." the phone whined. The app's robotic disapproval echoed her own cautious inner voice.

"Shut up," she muttered, a small rebellion sparking low in her belly.

The road meandered past older houses, their darkened windows hinting at private lives, secret intimacies. The dappled sunlight through the trees lent the scene an otherworldly shimmer that made her feel almost voyeuristic. And then she saw it: a vintage VW van, a glorious riot of faded psychedelic colors—swirling oranges, sunshine yellows, and deep ocean blues, all softened by years of sun and road trips. It was pulled haphazardly to the side of the road, one of its oversized tires slightly askew in the gravel. Beside it lay a young man with his legs sprawled out, jeans slung low on his hips, a tangle of tools scattered around him as he wrestled with the engine. His long, sun-streaked hair, thick with grease and sweat, fell across his furrowed brow, and the lean curve of his back as he strained over the engine sent a surge of illicit interest through Chloe. A small, faded peace sign sticker clung to the van's rear bumper, a testament to a different era, a different way of life.

Her foot instinctively eased off the accelerator, her gaze fixed on the scene. He looked up, catching her eye with a raw intensity that seemed to pierce through layers of her carefully constructed composure. Abandoning the stubborn engine, he pushed himself up with a slow, suggestive smirk.

"Lost, darlin'?" he drawled, his voice a low, gravelly sound that resonated deep within her, thick with a hint of something untamed and utterly free. He pushed himself fully upright, his gaze lingering on her body through the open car window, an unhurried, appreciative assessment that sent a flush racing to Chloe's cheeks. His eyes traced the line of her neck down to the swell of her breasts beneath her thin work blouse, as if charting a course to a more intimate destination.

He approached her car, his movements languid despite the grease staining his hands, the confident energy radiating from his body beckoning her toward the unknown. The scent of him as he drew closer—oil and hot metal mingling with the earthy aroma of the nearby woods and something inherently male—seemed to promise a different kind of adventure. She found herself reaching for the window switch, the sudden descent of the glass amplifying the chirping of unseen insects and the low pulse of his footsteps. He didn't ask if she needed help with directions. He leaned in, his arms resting on the doorframe, his gaze locking on to hers. "That turn felt . . . deliberate. What's the real destination you had in mind?"

Her eyes, betraying her, drifted to the colorful haven of his van, a space that felt worlds away from her sterile office. He opened the side door, revealing a surprisingly cozy interior—worn velvet cushions, scattered maps hinting at journeys taken, and the warm scent of sunbaked upholstery and something uniquely him. He gestured her inside, a silent invitation to leave her predictable life behind, even for a little while.

She didn't hesitate. She turned off her engine, the sudden silence heightening her anticipation. He took her hand, his calloused fingers gentle against her own as he led her to the van. The faded paint felt cool beneath her touch as she entered.

Inside, the air was thick with possibility. He turned to her, his gaze intense, and the world outside the van—the winding road, the setting sun—faded to a blurry backdrop. His hands, still bearing traces of grease, now tenderly cupped her face, his thumbs stroking her cheekbones. The kiss that followed was slow and intentional, a promise of deeper intimacy to come within the close confines of the interior. His lips were soft at first, then firm, demanding, coaxing hers apart until his tongue plunged in, exploring every sensitive curve of her mouth.

His hands slid down her body, tracing the contours of her spine before finding the hem of her work blouse. The pregnant hush inside the van was interrupted only by the rustle of chiffon as he gently pulled it free, then discarded it onto the worn cushions. His rough fingers glided over the silk of her camisole, then under it, finding the warm, yielding skin of her stomach. She shivered as he pushed the delicate garment higher. His eyes darkened as he took in her lace-covered breasts, then his head lowered, his mouth engulfing one yearning nipple through the fabric, suckling, teasing, until a raw moan escaped her. He stripped away her camisole, tossing it aside, then moved his mouth to her exposed skin. His tongue traced a path down her sternum, leaving a wet, hot trail, his teeth gently nipping at her ribs as his hands expertly worked the button of her skirt. The zipper hissed open, a forbidden sound in the quiet space, and the wool yielded to his tugging, collecting around her hips before pooling around her ankles on the worn floor. She kicked it away, impatient, her legs now bare save for the gossamer lace of her panties.

He knelt before her, his hands parting her thighs, pushing the soft fabric aside until she was completely exposed. His gaze devoured her, a feral, famished assessment that sent a thrill of anticipation through her. Then, slowly, deliberately, he lowered his head, his hot breath ghosting over her most sensitive flesh before his mouth buried itself in her, consuming her with a ferocity that stole her breath. His tongue flicked and swirled, a skilled artist tormenting her clitoris, drawing out every ounce of pleasure, every passion-filled gasp. His fingers plunged inside her, deep and demanding, stretching her, then withdrawing only to plunge again, a furious rhythm that drove her body into a ravenous, undulating convulsion against the cushions. The bliss became pain, an unbearable, escalating torture that pushed her further toward the edge of oblivion. Her hands tangled in his hair, pulling him closer, demanding more, even as she whimpered for respite.

He lifted his head, his face flushed, leaving her gasping, seared, undone. He wasted no time. With a swift movement, he pushed her back against the velvet cushions, his body following hers, pressing down until she was pinned beneath him. His erection, thick and throbbing, brushed powerfully against her entrance, a blunt, insistent demand. He teased her, pressing its weight against her slick center, letting her feel the promise of a complete, uninhibited union, before pulling back just an inch.

Chloe released a low moan, her hips jerking upward in a mute entreaty for him to finally enter. He met her hips with a hard, intensifying friction, the pressure building a cadence, denying the release she so eagerly craved. The air grew thick with the scent of their combined desire. The sounds of the outside world faded to a distant murmur; her blood pounded in her ears. She could feel the urgent presence of his form pressed against hers, an unspoken pledge signaling what was yet to come. Quivering, her core began to clench, her body poised on the edge, his escalating movements threatening to obliterate her senses in a blinding, silent explosion of agony and thrill. She was there, right there, trembling, flustered, about to break—

Suddenly, the low drone of her own car engine jolted Chloe back to the present. Exhaust fumes and stale air-conditioning replaced the earthy, intoxicating aroma of the van's interior. The dappled sunlight through the trees was still visible beyond her windshield, but the evocative filter was gone. The young man was outside, wrestling with his engine, a frustrated grunt escaping his lips. He hadn't moved toward her car, hadn't spoken suggestive words, hadn't opened the van door.

Chloe's grip tightened on the steering wheel, her breath catching in her throat, a potent wave of longing washing over her. Her body hummed with a persistent vibration that echoed the impotent idle of her car's engine. With a sigh, she pressed the accelerator, the image of the faded VW van shrinking in her rearview mirror. The GPS, bless its oblivious heart, directed her back to the familiar highway, unaware of the intimate journey her imagination had just taken.

CHAPTER 2

Bianca

Bianca's thumb hovered over her phone screen, the cool glass, a stark contrast to the heat that had been simmering within her all evening. Another Saturday night was unfolding in the predictable quiet of her home, the curated displays of other people's supposed bliss on social media only underscoring the growing sense of . . . beige that had settled over her reality with Mark. From behind the closed door of their bedroom, his contented snoring provided a soundtrack to her restless scrolling.

Then, as if summoned by her unspoken desires, an unknown profile detonated on her feed: "Rogue_Ink." Even the name felt like a transgression. His profile picture was a close-up, almost confrontational, of heavily tattooed knuckles gripping a black motorcycle throttle, the starkly defined veins in his forearms hinting at a raw, physical power. There was an unapologetic masculinity in the image, a rebellious edge that snapped Bianca from her digital stupor.

Her click was immediate, almost a visceral reaction, like reaching for forbidden fruit. His bio was a single, defiant line, etched in a stark-white font against a black background: "Ride hard. Live raw. Leave a mark." His photos were an assault on her senses: the hint of an inked chest beneath the ripped edges of a worn leather vest, piercing blue eyes that seemed to bore right through the screen, a knowing smirk that promised a kind of delicious trouble Bianca hadn't encountered in years.

A dangerous curiosity, sharp and insistent, coiled low in Bianca's gut. She followed him, a covert act of revolt against her Saturday night reality. The follow-back was instantaneous. A nervous thrill skittered across her skin.

His first message arrived like a surge of electricity: *What's the wildest thing you've ever wanted?*

Bianca's breath hitched in her throat. Her fingers trembled as she typed a carefully veiled response, her mind already racing down forbidden paths. The glow of her bedroom lamp throbbed with a sudden illicit energy, the silence foregrounding the beating of her own heart. Her virtual connection with this enigmatic stranger, this "Rogue_Ink," was already more potent, more alive, than any physical touch she'd experienced with Mark in what felt like an eternity.

The subsequent messages became a dance of innuendo and daring, each carefully chosen word igniting a more vivid, more urgent scenario in Bianca's mind. The rough texture of his tattooed hands against her bare skin, the intense focus of his cobalt eyes locking on to hers, the low, gravelly timbre she imagined his voice would possess—it all coalesced into a burning need for a real-life encounter, an unfulfilled ache to bridge the digital divide.

Emboldened by the anonymity of the internet, Bianca typed a message, her fingers flying across the screen with a newfound recklessness: *Want to video call sometime? See if the reality matches the pixels?* She held her breath, a knot of anticipation tightening in her stomach.

Minutes stretched, the silence in her bedroom amplifying the drumming of her heartbeat. Finally, a message alert chimed, breaking the tense quiet. *Now?*

Bianca's heart hammered against her ribs, a wild, untamed melody synchronized with the persona of the man on her screen. A thrill surged through her. Without a second thought, she tapped the video call icon, her attention fixed on the screen as it began to connect.

His face filled her view, larger than life, the blue of his eyes even more mesmerizing in motion, a real-time smirk playing around his lips as he leaned closer to the camera. His dark hair was slightly disheveled, falling across his forehead in a way that felt both dangerous and alluring, and the tantalizing glimpse of a heavily tatted shoulder beneath the worn black fabric of his T-shirt sent a wave of liquid fire through Bianca.

He didn't speak, just held her gaze with an unnerving intensity that made her breath catch in her throat. Bianca found herself mirroring his unspoken challenge, her own eyes locking with his, a silent battle of wills and burgeoning desire. The silence stretched, thick with unspoken promises and the weight of mutual arousal.

Then, with a slow, deliberate movement, Bianca's hand, suddenly feeling alien and disconnected from her usual demureness, slipped beneath the soft silk of her pajama top, her fingertips tracing the sensitive curve of her breast. Rogue_Ink's gaze dropped instantly, a flicker of something instinctive, dominant, in the depths of his blue eyes. He mimicked her actions, his own tattooed hand disappearing from view below the frame of his camera.

A silent, erotic ballet began, their flushed faces illuminated by the glow of their respective screens. Bianca's fingers teased and tormented her nipples, the friction building a delicious throbbing deep within her. A low moan, involuntary and revealing, escaped her lips, the sound amplified by the sudden intimacy of the video call. She reached for the vibrator on her nightstand.

On her screen, Bianca could see the flexing of Rogue_Ink's jaw muscles, the beads of sweat forming on his forehead as he focused intently on her. The masterful sounds emanating from his end, though muffled, broadcasted his delight through the airwaves, paralleling her own escalating excitement.

The tension mounted with each shared glance, each stolen touch, each ragged breath that filled the virtual air between them, fueling a mutual arousal that felt both forbidden and utterly irresistible. Bianca's breath came in short, sharp gasps as the toy pulsed against her most sensitive flesh, the sensation building to an unbearable intensity, threatening to consume her. Her vision tunneled as her hips began to grind against the mattress. Her fingers clenched the vibrator, forcing the insistent hum deeper, driving her higher, past thought, past sensation, toward oblivion. Every nerve ending in her body flared, screaming for release. The energy coiled tight in her core, vibrating outward, threatening to explode. She was on the apex, her being throbbing with unbearable pressure, poised to detonate in a silent, all-consuming convulsion . . .

Just as the first powerful waves of her orgasm began to ripple through her body, a new-message alert chimed on her phone. Her eyes flickered down, the glowing notification displaying a message from Rogue_Ink:

ROGUE_INK: *Yeah, I'd be into Face Timing.*

The casual, almost nonchalant, and clearly delayed response slammed into Bianca's consciousness like a bucket of ice water. The pulsing of her vibrator suddenly felt jarring, almost clinical, as the intense heat in her body cooled and the reality of their asynchronous interaction crashed over her with brutal force.

The image of Rogue_Ink on her screen, his face still contorted in a moment of private fervor, seemed suddenly distant, a carefully constructed persona existing only within the confines of her phone. The seductive glow of the screen evaporated, her gateway to unleashed desire collapsing as the device stared back at her blankly, a harsh reminder of the chasm that online connection could not bridge. A restless tingle, the ghost of a promised sensation, lingered in her core, resonating with the monotony of Mark's snoring.

The void that gnawed at her seemed only to have deepened.

CHAPTER 3

Clara

The stark white of the unpaid bills scattered across the polished kitchen counter served as a sterile testament to the slow erosion of passion within Clara's marriage to Ben. His side of their king-sized bed remained stubbornly cool each night, his soft snores a nightly soundtrack to her own restless heat, an insistent purring of unsatisfied desires that kept her teetering on the edge of wakefulness. Their intimacy had devolved into a predictable, almost perfunctory routine, a pale imitation of the wildfire that had once consumed their early years, which was now neatly filed away in the dusty archives of "responsible adult" life.

But over the past few days, a series of increasingly bold and explicit notes had begun to appear at Clara's workplace. Tucked beneath papers on her desk, slipped into her mailbox, left within the pages of a well-worn novel in the faculty lounge—each note felt like a forbidden touch in the sterile environment of her professional life. Today, as she reached for her usual double latte at the Daily Grind, welcoming the warmth of the ceramic mug against her palm, she felt fingers brushing her free hand with a deliberate assertiveness that sent a shiver of fear and thrill down her spine. A small, tightly folded note materialized in her grasp, containing a simple message: *I'm watching.*

Clara's breath hitched in her throat, the rich aroma of roasted coffee suddenly feeling thick and cloying. Her gaze, which had been fixed on the friendly barista, finally lifted, drawn by an almost magnetic force. And then she saw him.

He was leaning casually against the magazine rack near the exit, the dim lighting of the coffee shop casting sharp shadows across his angular features. His eyes, dark and intense, locked on hers with a piercing focus that made her heart pound against her ribs. The slow, knowing curl of his lip rearranged his features into an expression both dangerous and undeniably alluring. The air between them crackled with an immediate, almost violent sexual tension. His eyes held hers captive, an unspoken vow of the things he wanted to do to her.

The bustling coffee shop dissolved. The sounds of the espresso machine faded, replaced by a profound silence. The scent of roasted beans morphed into the comforting, slightly dusty fragrance of aged paper and leather-bound books. She found herself no longer standing in the queue but in the quiet of a dimly lit bookstore, the towering shelves casting long, intriguing shadows. He gestured silently with a tilt of his head toward the back, and she followed, her sensible work heels clicking softly on the polished concrete floor, the sound echoing in the stillness. They moved deeper into the labyrinth of literature, down a narrow, deserted aisle lined with lofty shelves filled with forgotten tales and untold secrets. The only illumination came from a single, bare bulb at the far end of the aisle, casting an almost theatrical light.

His gaze intensified as he watched her walk ahead, the subtle sway of her skirt—a soft, flowing linen that brushed against her calves with each step—signaling a silent invitation. As she reached the shadowed end of the aisle, the scent of old paper suddenly stronger, he was there, impossibly close behind her, the heat radiating from his body a palpable presence against her back. A thrill of anticipation, sharp and undeniable, coursed through her, mixing with a delicious tremor of fear.

His hands, strong and sure, slid around her waist, his fingers, the backs hinting at the intricate artwork beneath his skin, reaching beneath the smooth hem of her skirt. The cool air against her bare skin sent a rush of unfiltered awareness through her. He lifted the fabric slowly, deliberately, the whisper of the linen against her thighs a sensual friction that accentuated the silence of the empty aisle. His lips pressed against the sensitive nape of her neck, his breath hot and moist against her skin as his hands moved higher, cupping her buttocks with a commanding grip that brooked no argument. The pressure was firm, insistent, pulling her closer against the hard lines of his body. A low moan, a sound she barely recognized as her own, fractured the quiet of the bookstore, the anticipation coiling tighter and tighter, building toward a fever pitch. She leaned back, the solid presence of his chest against her spine igniting a storm of sensation. His fingers began to explore the curve of her hip, dipping lower, tracing the seam of her stockings with a deliberate slowness that was both agonizing and exquisite. The scent of old paper and his own earthy musk filled her senses.

He spun her gently, pressing her against the soaring shelves, the cool, rough spines of vintage books a stark contrast to the burning heat consuming her. His mouth descended on hers, leaving her breathless, tasting of urgency and illicit desire. His tongue dueled with hers, an untamed invasion that ignited a wildfire in her core. His hands, never still, moved beneath her skirt again, swiftly dispatching the delicate lace of her panties, allowing them to fall silently to the floor.

He knelt before her, pushing her legs apart with a firm hand, his gaze never leaving her flushed face. The bare bulb at the end of the aisle illuminated her exposed center, making her feel utterly vulnerable, utterly desired. His fingers, strong and calloused, parted her slick folds, finding her clitoris with unerring precision. He began to stroke it, pressing, circling, teasing, then plunging deep inside her, stretching her, exploring her intimate depths with a ferocity that made her entire body tremble. Clara gasped, her head thrown back against the rough texture of the books, her fingers digging into the dust jacket of a forgotten tome. Each movement drove her higher, an unbearable gratification that bordered on pain, pulling her deeper into the swirling vortex of sensation.

His mouth descended once more, his hot breath ghosting over her sensitive flesh before his tongue flicked out, tasting her, consuming her with a fierce passion. He suckled and licked, driving her to the final explosive moments, pushing her toward the rapture she craved. Her hips began to grind against his face, an unconscious dance begging for the release he so expertly withheld. The pressure intensified, building to a suffocating crescendo, every nerve ending screaming.

Then, with a sudden, forceful motion, he lifted her, pinning her against the tall bookshelf. Her legs instinctively wrapped around his waist, her skirt hiking up, bunching around her hips. The rough edges of the old books pressed into her back, a strange, thrilling counterpoint to the soft skin of her thighs wrapped around him. His hands braced her, one on her hip, the other sliding to cup her backside, lifting her just a fraction. His heavy erection, thick and throbbing, pressed firmly against her entrance, a bold, undeniable presence. He let her feel the distended shape of him, the agonizing promise of complete fullness, then he pulled back just enough to create a searing friction.

Clara arched against him, unable to speak, her body convulsing with a guttural plea. Her hips bucked against his, demanding his entry. He pressed his body against hers in slow motion, a solid, mounting pressure, refusing to grant the culmination her body begged for. The air in the silent aisle grew taut with the scent of their shared passion, and the world dissolved into the deafening thrum of her own blood and the raw friction his movements created. She could feel the crushing weight of his desire, a scorching presence against her most sensitive curves, driving her to the point of no return. An internal grip took hold, her body poised on the edge, her soul threatening to ignite in a radiant inferno of pure sensation.

The sharp, unexpected clatter of a ceramic mug hitting the tiled floor shattered the intense silence. Clara blinked, her focus snapping back to the bustling coffee shop. The man was still leaning against the magazine rack, his dark eyes fixed on hers, that same knowing curl of his lip playing on his mouth. The feel of his hands, the hushed intimacy of the bookstore aisle, and the intoxicating scent of old paper and forbidden desire all vanished, catapulting her back to the mundane reality of her morning coffee run with a lingering heat in her belly and a tremor in her throat.

CHAPTER 4

Ava

Ava felt the familiar burn of frustration, a slow, simmering heat that threatened to breach the carefully constructed walls of her professional composure. Years of unwavering dedication, countless late nights fueled by lukewarm coffee, and the innovative ideas that often seemed to blossom solely within her subjective reality usually vanished into the bureaucratic ether of Sterling Corp. The only consistent exception was Julian Thorne.

Julian Thorne. His name alone carried the palpable weight of power. He was sharp, brilliant, and possessed a gaze that could dissect a balance sheet or, in the charged moments she allowed herself, strip her bare with equal precision. He was her mentor . . . and the object of her simmering, intensely inappropriate desire.

During their intense one-on-one meetings, his eyes would sometimes linger on her for a fraction too long, a flicker of something unreadable in their depths that sent a flash of pure awareness through her.

Her recurring imaginations during these meetings were a perilous venture. His hand, usually firm on a report, would suddenly reach across his large, polished mahogany desk to cup her cheek. The conversation would shift, the corporate jargon replaced by hushed confessions. His gaze would lift from the spreadsheets and home in on her lips. His voice, normally rigidly controlled, would drop to a low murmur as he spoke of her hidden strengths and the undeniable pull he felt.

The moments she imagined often centered on stolen time after hours. The hum of the ventilation system would be their only soundtrack, the cool leather of his executive chair a silent invitation. His hands would explore her body, his fingers sliding beneath her skirt, pressing against her back, squeezing her breasts . . .

Today, during a strategy session, Julian's gaze locked with hers. She could see that flicker in his eyes, and for a split second, her desire eclipsed her mind. She heard him dismiss the rest of the room with a curt wave, his focus solely on her. Then he rose and walked toward her, the tension thick.

Instead of stopping beside her chair, however, he continued past, his gaze never leaving hers, until he reached his imposing desk. With a slow, deliberate movement, he leaned against the edge, his knuckles white as he gripped the polished wood. The implicit invitation hung heavy in the air, thick with the scent of his expensive cologne and the barely suppressed energy between them.

Ava rose, drawn by an invisible thread. Her steps were hesitant at first, then gained a strange sense of inevitability as she moved toward him. The expanse of the desk separated them, its polished surface gleaming under the recessed office lighting, a barrier that felt both significant and utterly meaningless in the face of their unspoken want.

Without a word, Julian's powerful hands reached out, grasping her hips with a firmness that sent sparks rushing through her. He lifted her with surprising ease, the suddenness of the action stealing her breath, and effortlessly placed her on the smooth surface of his desk. The sleek wood pressed against the backs of her thighs through the thin fabric of her tailored skirt, the unexpected coolness accentuating the sudden heat flaring within her.

His gaze burned into hers. Her blood pounded in her ears. He leaned closer, the scent of sandalwood and something sharper, more intimately him, filling her senses. One hand remained grasping her hip, his thumb pressing into the small of her back, while the other reached out, his long fingers tracing the delicate line of her throat down to the notch at its base. The subtle rasp of his fingertips against her skin, the barely contained tremor in his touch, mirrored her own escalating arousal.

The air thrummed with anticipation. All she could hear was the accelerated fluttering of her own breathing and the low, insistent humming deep within her. His hand left her throat, dipping lower, his fingers finding the hem of her skirt once more. This time, there was no hesitation. He lifted the fabric, revealing the tops of her stockinged thighs, his gaze following the upward sweep of his hand, a burning intensity in his dark eyes.

His fingers, gentle despite their inherent strength, traced the sensitive skin of her inner thigh, moving ever closer to the core of her desire. A low moan, a sound she barely recognized, escaped her lips. The pressure against her back increased as he leaned in further, his lips hovering just above hers, his breath warm against her skin. She could almost taste him, the forbidden sweetness a tantalizing promise. The hum of the ventilation system seemed to grow louder, vibrating in time with the beating of her heart.

Then, with a slow, deliberate movement, he hiked her skirt higher, bunching the fabric around her waist. His eyes, dark with obsession, devoured her exposed lace panties. His fingers, firm and unerring, slipped beneath the delicate fabric, parting her with a single, territorial slide. He found her immediately, slick and throbbing, and began to stroke her with relentless, driving force. Ava gasped, her body arching into his touch, her hands bracing against his broad shoulders. He circled, pressed, and teased, driving her higher, pushing her to the tipping point of an unbearable fulfillment that bordered on agony. The cool, hard surface of the desk against her back amplified every exquisite sensation.

He leaned in, his lips brushing against her ear, whispering guttural urgings she couldn't quite decipher; she could only understand the raw desire behind them. With a sudden, surprising shift, he pulled her to the very edge of the desk so that her legs dangled freely, leaving her completely exposed to his gaze. His own body pressed between her legs, his erection, thick and pulsing, brushing provocatively against her entrance, a bold, insistent challenge. He let her feel the distended shape of him, the agonizing promise of complete fullness, then he pulled back just an inch, creating a searing friction that made her whimper.

Ava let out a sharp, breathless gasp, her hips jerking, a silent plea for him to finally enter. He began a tantalizing motion that had her whole body begging for more, his demanding, insistent presence intensifying her agitation, holding her just short of the release she so profoundly needed. The air in the quiet office grew heavy with the scent of their mingled desire, and the world narrowed to the deafening beat of her own blood and the sharp, exhilarating friction his movements were creating. She could feel the insistence of his form pressed against her, an undeniable promise of what was yet to come, propelling her toward the culmination of her desire. Her body's core constricted, quivering, threatening to rupture her very essence. Her entire being was a fuse, lit and burning down to its end, poised to burst forth in a profound, uncontained release.

Just as the powerful ripples began to build, just as the edge of climax felt tantalizingly close, the sharp, distinct sound of Julian clearing his throat broke the silence of the actual conference room. Ava blinked, her focus snapping back to the present. Julian was still seated at the head of the table, his gaze now directed at the presentation on the screen, a slight, almost imperceptible frown creasing his brow as he waited for her input. The lingering heat in her body, the distraught beating of her heart, and the phantom ache between her legs faded, replaced by the mundane furnishings of the room and the stark, cold surface of his desk.

CHAPTER 5

Seraphina

S eraphina's throat was tight, the lukewarm beer doing nothing to soothe the sudden dryness that had spread south. Karaoke night at the Rusty Mug was her weekly dose of vicarious living, allowing her to watch others unleash their inner divas while she remained safely in the shadows. Tonight, Maya, fueled by tequila and a reckless spirit, had other, far more invasive plans.

"Sera! You gotta! Just one song! For me!" Maya's drunken tug propelled Seraphina toward the garishly lit stage, a spotlight suddenly pinning her like a startled insect. Before she could form a coherent protest, Maya was slurring to the DJ about a duet.

Then he looked at her. Leaning against the speaker, a microphone swinging from his fingers, he exuded a potent, almost commanding charisma. His dark eyes locked onto Seraphina's, a slow, knowing smirk spreading across his lips as if he could already taste the forbidden fruit she represented. "Looks like we're making music, sweetheart," his voice rumbled, a low vibration that resonated deep in Seraphina's body, stirring a heat she rarely acknowledged.

The possessive drawl, the way his gaze lingered, tracing the line of her collarbone down to the swell of her breasts beneath her thin top, ignited a sensation so immediately and carnal it made her thighs clench, a humid warmth blooming between her legs. Every nerve ending felt suddenly alive, buzzing with an anticipation that bordered on pain.

As the music for the sultry duet began, a nervous energy crackled between them. During a break in the lyrics, Seraphina mumbled an excuse about needing the restroom, the words catching in her dry throat. As she turned away, he followed, his presence a palpable heat behind her in the crowded hallway, a magnetic pull she couldn't resist. Before she reached the bathroom door, his hand closed around her arm, his grip surprisingly firm yet sending a surge straight to her core, igniting a tremor that spread through her limbs.

He turned her to face him, his dark eyes intense, devouring her. "That song . . ." he murmured, his breath warm against her ear, a delicious invasion that sent shivers down her spine. "It felt . . . personal."

Seraphina's heart hammered against her ribs, a hysterical hummingbird trapped in a cage. The confined space of the hallway, the low murmur of voices from the bar, the raw intensity of his gaze—it all heightened the forbidden desire rising within her, encroaching on her solitary existence. She felt him lean closer, his lips, full and dangerous, brushing against hers, promising a stolen, frenzied kiss in this liminal space, a secret shared between only them before the world reclaimed them. The air around them thickened, heavy with unspoken desire, the tension almost unbearable.

They found their way back onstage just in time, and his hand reached to guide her to the microphone, lingering on her waist, his thumb pressing into the small of her back, a wordless pledge of deeper exploration later, a direct line to the emptiness within her. Their voices intertwined, the lyrics about secret desires now representing a thinly veiled, intimate conversation between them. His body heat radiated toward her like a delicious torrent, pulling her further into his seduction.

As they sang about stolen kisses in the dark, Seraphina felt herself beginning to collapse under his spell, fueled by the lingering imprint of his touch. She felt their mouths meeting, not under the bright lights of the stage but in the shadows of the parking lot—a hungry claiming, hands fumbling with clothes, urgency overriding all pretense. The thought alone sent a shock wave through her, leaving her breathless.

The applause at the end of their song was deafening, a roaring wave that seemed to push them closer. Afterward, he bought her a drink at the crowded bar, his leg brushing hers under the table, a deliberate, electrifying contact that made her gasp. Double entendres and unspoken invitations laced their conversation, feeding their raw attraction. Every shared glance, every knowing smile acknowledged the inevitable, an unspoken call to surrender.

Later, as they walked toward her car, the night air was crisp and carried a hint of frost, a stark contrast to the inferno raging inside Seraphina. "It's freezing." She shivered, pulling her jacket tighter, though the chill barely registered against the heat of her skin.

He nodded, his gaze intense, a consuming gleam in his dark eyes. "Hop in. We can . . . continue the conversation where it's warmer." His voice, a low rumble, bypassed her ears and went straight to the core of her, melting any last shred of resistance. Her hand was already reaching for the door handle, her body buzzing.

Inside the closed confines of her car, the air immediately felt charged and intimate, thick with unspoken promise.

The dim glow of the dashboard illuminated their faces, highlighting the hungry glint in his eyes as he turned to her, his knee nudging hers, a tantalizing pressure. The casual banter faded, replaced by a palpable, urgent tension that stretched taut between them. He reached out, his fingers tracing the line of her jaw, his thumb brushing her lower lip, his touch sending shivers down her spine that had nothing to do with the cold.

Their lips met, tentatively at first, a soft exploration, then with a raw eagerness. The kiss deepened, tongues tangling, tasting of whiskey and forbidden desire. The small space suddenly felt intensely personal and private, a cocoon from the outside world. His hand moved from her jaw to the nape of her neck, his fingers tangling in her hair as he pulled her closer, molding her body against his.

Seraphina's own hands found their way to his chest, feeling the hard beat of his heart beneath his shirt. The fabric felt thin, and the urge to touch his bare skin, to experience the warmth of his flesh against hers, was a sudden, almost overwhelming need. Their kiss grew more urgent, more demanding, his groan vibrating against her lips. Her fingers fumbled with the buttons of his shirt, hurried to peel away the layers, to unleash the raw passion simmering between them. He broke the kiss, his eyes still dark with hunger, and in one fluid motion unbuckled his seat belt.

"Move to the back," he rasped, his gaze fixed on her. Seraphina didn't hesitate. She scrambled over the console, her breath catching as he followed, the small space becoming even more impossibly tight, forcing their bodies flush against each other. Clothes became an immediate obstacle. His hands were everywhere, fumbling with the hem of her skirt, then pushing it up, fingers brushing against the silk of her panties. She helped him, clamoring, her own hands yanking at his belt, the sound of the buckle echoing loudly in the sudden quiet of the car. The seats were hard and awkward, but their urgency made it irrelevant. His mouth found her neck, then trailed lower, leaving a hot path across her skin as he explored the sensitive curve of her collarbone. She arched into him, an unspoken entreaty for more, for everything.

Then his fingers, hot and deliberate, slipped under the elastic of her panties. A sharp gasp escaped her, lost in the heavy air. His thumb found her clit, circling, pressing, rubbing with agonizing precision. Seraphina's hips began to move of their own accord, grinding into his hand, a wordless, insistent demand for more, for faster. Her breath hitched, ragged and shallow. The friction built, a delicious torment, pushing her higher. Her vision blurred; her ears filled with the roaring of blood in her veins as his expert fingers coaxed her closer to that ultimate, volcanic eruption. Spasms started deep inside her, building, threatening to shatter her into a million ecstatic pieces. The windows began to fog rapidly, a visual testament to the rising, suffocating heat within, the air thick with the scent of aroused bodies and raw anticipation. She could feel the hard ridge of him against her, pulsing, ready. Her body screamed for release.

A sudden, blinding flash of headlights cut through the darkness. Seraphina blinked, a worried gasp escaping her lips. The world snapped back into focus with a disorienting lurch. She was standing outside her car, her hand hovering near the door handle, the night air crisp against her skin. He was right beside her, his hand still on the doorframe, his eyes just as dark but glinting merely with polite inquiry, not the insatiable hunger of moments ago.

"So, ready to get warm?" he asked, his voice a casual rumble, completely devoid of the throaty rasp that had commanded her to the back seat.

The heat that had consumed her vanished, replaced by a sudden, jarring chill. The scent of him, the feel of his skin, the ghost of his caress all faded away, leaving her in the cold with the faint scent of stale beer and the embarrassing reality of her own frightened, ragged breathing. Her body reverberated with a lingering mania. The headlights passed, leaving her once again in the dim privacy of the parking lot, but the magic was irrevocably broken. It had all been in her head.

With a resigned sigh, her grasp loosened, slipping from the doorframe, the sudden emptiness within her far colder than the night itself.

CHAPTER 6

Isolde

Isolde moved through the pristine whiteness of the gallery, the polite murmurs of the art crowd fading to a distant hum. Her focus was solely on him, the artist, Kaelen. His energy was a palpable force, a raw magnetism surpassing the intellectual impact of his work, and it had settled deep in her core, resurrecting a forgotten part of her soul. When his intense eyes, deep pools of molten obsidian, locked on hers across the room, it wasn't merely an acknowledgment; it was a claiming, a silent, consuming declaration. A forbidden heat flared instantly within Isolde, spreading like wildfire through her veins, igniting every dormant nerve ending. It was a dangerous, intoxicating rush, the first hit of a potent drug.

He moved toward her, a commanding glint in his gaze that promised both danger and exquisite arousal. His approach was slow, deliberate, like that of a connoisseur savoring his most prized acquisition. "You see more than the surface," he growled, his voice a deep, resonant rumble that seemed to bypass her ears and settle directly in the space between her thighs. "Come. I have something to show you. Something . . . private." The invitation was a whisper, yet it roared through her internal realm, demanding immediate surrender.

He led her away from the curated displays, the hushed reverence of the main gallery melting away as they ventured down a narrow hallway where the air grew thick with the heady scent of turpentine and linseed oil, an elemental aroma that stirred something deep within Isolde, a forgotten wildness. He unlocked a heavy wooden door, the creak of the hinges, a dramatic prelude, revealing a small, dimly lit room. Canvases leaned against every wall, their surfaces alive with intensely erotic scenes—tangled limbs slick with sweat, faces contorted in exquisite agony, wild depictions of desire that made Isolde's breath catch in her throat, her own body responding with a sudden humid warmth. This was the artist's sanctuary, a space where his truest, most carnal visions took form, a temple to unbridled sensuality.

"My true muses," Kaelen said, his gaze sweeping over the explicit artwork before settling back on Isolde, his eyes burning into hers, a silent challenge. "They whisper their secrets onto the canvas. And now . . . you." This wasn't just a request that she model for him; it was an initiation into his most intimate world, a realm where the boundaries between art and raw desire dissolved into a potent, intoxicating blend, a dangerous fusion that promised ultimate sensation.

His fingers, stained with vibrant crimson and deep indigo, reached out, not for charcoal but to trace the sharp lines of Isolde's collarbone. His touch was light, all-encompassing, a feather-light brush that left a trail of fire in its wake. "Your skin," he murmured, his thumb stroking the sensitive curve of her neck, sending a spark of kinetic energy through her, making her muscles clench, her breath hitch. "It's a canvas wanting to be marked." The words were a promise, a threat, a seductive command.

The air in the secret room throbbed with unspoken lust, thick and heavy like summer air before a storm. Isolde felt a visceral need to be touched, to be consumed by this intense, uninhibited man and the raw energy of his artistic space. The graphic artwork surrounding them seemed to spark a shared, unspoken need, urging her deeper into the intoxicating haze. She salivated for the next hit.

He pulled her closer, the scent of paint and his own musky masculinity filling her senses, stealing her breath, making her lightheaded with desire. His hands, those artist's hands that could capture the most fleeting expressions of ecstasy on canvas, explored every inch of her body, mapping its contours as if she were his next masterpiece, a living, breathing sculpture drowning in a flood of sensation.

Kaelen stepped closer, his body heat radiating against hers, a furnace against her suddenly chilled skin. He didn't speak, his eyes doing all the talking as they devoured her, lingering on the swell of her breasts beneath her silk blouse, the curve of her hips beneath her fitted skirt, stripping her bare with his gaze alone.

He reached out again, this time his fingers tangling in the hair at the nape of her neck, tilting her head back, exposing the vulnerable curve of her throat. His lips brushed against her ear, his breath hot and urgent, sending shivers racing down her spine. "Tell me," he whispered, his low voice vibrating through her bones, "what colors are you hiding beneath that elegant surface? What sensations are you craving?"

Isolde's breath hitched, a sharp, unbidden intake of air. The question was a direct assault on her carefully constructed composure, shattering it into a million glittering fragments. A powerful compulsion surged within her to shed the polite exterior and reveal the raw, uninhibited desires Kaelen's art and his gaze had so expertly unearthed. The secret room, with its explicit depictions of sensuality, felt like a permission slip, a space where those hidden colors could finally be unleashed.

His mouth descended, claiming hers in a brutal, hungry kiss that left her reeling. His tongue plunged, mimicking the invasion her body craved, tasting of turpentine, raw passion, and the promise of ultimate surrender. Her hands, trembling, clawed at his shirt, desperate to feel the warmth of his skin, to tear away the barriers between them. He responded with equal ferocity, his fingers fumbling with the delicate buttons of her silk blouse, tearing them off in his haste. The cool air was a shock against her exposed skin, quickly replaced by the scorching heat of his hands as they cupped her breasts, his thumbs circling her hardened nipples, sending thrills of enjoyment through her.

A low moan escaped her throat as he pushed her gently back against a canvas-covered wall, the rough texture a delicious contrast to the smooth heat of his mouth now trailing down her neck, across her collarbone, and finally to the valley between her breasts. She arched her back, offering herself, thirsty for more. He pulled her skirt up, his fingers brushing the sensitive skin of her inner thigh, making her gasp. The air was thick with the scent of their combined arousal, a heady perfume of paint, sweat, and raw desire. He lifted her, wrapping her legs around his waist, pressing her against the hard ridge of his erection, a pulsing demand against her most sensitive core. She could feel the heat, the pressure, the promise of imminent release. Her body screamed for him, for the ultimate plunge, for the complete, mind-numbing release that hovered just out of reach. Her inner muscles clenched, a rhythmic tightening, pulling her closer and closer to the point of unraveling.

The sharp, insistent ringing of a phone pierced the haze. Isolde blinked, her eyes snapping open, a sudden, disorienting chill washing over her. She was standing in the dimly lit secret room, her hand still resting on the heavy wooden door, her silk blouse still perfectly buttoned, her skirt unrumpled. The art studio scent of turpentine and linseed oil no longer felt primitive. The erotic canvases on the walls were just paintings, their raw depictions now merely inert images. Kaelen was across the room, his back to her, holding a small, sleek phone to his ear, his expression, calm and professional. The intense glint in his eyes was gone, replaced by a distant politeness as he murmured into the receiver.

A desolate chill settled in her core, an emptiness far more profound than the night air.

CHAPTER 7

Lena

The 7:15 a.m. train was Lena's daily cattle car, a sardine tin of barely conscious bodies pressed together. Usually she retreated into her headphones, a sonic barrier against the unwanted intimacy, the unwelcome brush of strangers. But then there was him.

He always boarded at the same godforsaken stop, a sculpted silhouette in a suit that screamed power and blatant disregard for the sweaty discomfort of public transport. His dark eyes, the color of a stormfront gathering over an unforgiving sea, would sweep through the car, his gaze consuming everything in its path. And when those eyes snagged on Lena's, it wasn't a polite glance, not a casual acknowledgment. It was a visceral, fierce stare that felt like a physical touch, stripping away her professional demeanor layer by agonizing layer, igniting a forbidden inferno low in her belly.

Lena knew nothing of him beyond the relentless intensity in his eyes and the way his presence made her thighs clench, a humid warmth spreading between her legs. Yet as she sat trapped in the hypnotic sway of the train day after day, an obsession so raw and explicit that it threatened to consume her waking hours had taken root, blurring the lines between reality and reverie.

In her private reality, the jostling bodies would vanish, dissolving like smoke, the screech of the tracks fading. Only the two of them would remain, cocooned in a bubble of insatiable longing, the air thick with unvoiced lust. His gaze wouldn't just linger; it would devour her, tracing the outline of her breasts beneath her crisp work blouse, seeking out the dark promise of her nipples. Descending lower, it would linger on the way her skirt rode up slightly as she sat, revealing a sliver of inner thigh . . .

Her need became a persistent feature of her daily commute. She would feel him moving down the aisle, a powerful force, his hand deliberately brushing against her thigh, the casual contact sending a powerful shock wave directly to her core, making her gasp. The accidental press of bodies during sudden stops would set the stage for clandestine connection, his hard frame molding against hers, his groin pressing blatantly, insistently against her belly. She would feel the fabric of his expensive suit trousers stretch thin against the rigid heat of him, creating an excruciating friction. His eyes would lock on to hers, promising the kind of raw, no-holds-barred encounter she secretly craved, stripping away every inhibition. The unspoken language between them was pure sexual energy, a mutual understanding of an impulse that demanded to be fed.

His scent, a mix of expensive cologne, clean linen, and male musk, filled her senses, a suffocating sweetness that left her lightheaded. She imagined his fingers, strong and sure, tracing the delicate curve of her ankle, then sliding slowly upward, beneath the hem of her skirt, his touch burning a trail along her calf, her knee, toward the soft skin of her inner thigh. Every brush, every subtle shift of his body against hers in the crowded space sent a fresh wave of fire through her, intensifying her need.

The most potent moments culminated during those jarring halts, when the train lurched and their bodies slammed together with delicious force. She felt his hand, ostensibly for balance, settling on her hip, his fingers digging in, pulling her closer until the hard ridge of his erection pressed against her, a relentless, throbbing demand. Their gazes would lock, a silent, unrestrained understanding passing between them—acknowledgment of a shared, forbidden desire that the confines of the train only amplified. His breath, hot and ragged, brushed against her ear as his head dipped, his lips almost touching her temple, the promise of a deeper taste tormentingly close. She felt his hips move, a subtle, deliberate grind against her, his rigid heat driving her insane. The world narrowed to just them, the vibrating steel, their mirrored panting breaths.

Today, as the train screeched to an unexpected, violent stop, his body slammed against hers, sending a shock wave through her. The blatant pressure of him was unmistakable, undeniable. His eyes, inches from hers, held a feral, insatiable intensity, a silent promise of what awaited them beyond the mundane reality of the commute, beyond the thin fabric separating their urgent flesh. The world dissolved into a single, overwhelming sensation: the pressing heat, the friction, the dizzying surge toward release.

Then, impossibly, his hand slipped farther. Unseen, unheard amid the crush of bodies, his fingers found the soft, yielding skin beneath her skirt. A gasp caught in Lena's throat, swallowed by the roar of the train. His thumb brushed against the delicate fabric of her panties, then slipped beneath, seeking, finding. Every brush of his fingers, precise and deliberate, sent lightning bolts through her, straight to her core. The friction increased, a teasing, building pressure, driving her higher and higher. Her hips began an unconscious sway, an insistent undulation against his demanding touch, silently begging him for more. The air around them crackled, thick with the scent of aroused bodies and raw, uninhibited lust. He was mapping her every peak, every valley, pushing her relentlessly toward the edge. Her vision blurred and her ears filled with the roaring of blood in her veins as his expert fingers coaxed her closer and closer to that ultimate, seismic climax. The electricity started deep inside, building, promising to unravel her completely, but the final, shattering sensation remained tantalizingly, frustratingly out of reach.

"Doors opening! Last stop, Downtown Station!"

The automated voice booming through the car speakers pierced the haze. Lena's eyes snapped open. She was sitting upright, her back pressed against the uncomfortable plastic seat. Her headphones, still on, played a soft jazz melody. Her skirt was unrumpled, her blouse neat. The man stood several feet away, perfectly composed, his hand resting casually on a pole as the train doors hissed open. He glanced over, his expression neutral, and gave her a polite nod before turning to exit the train, merging seamlessly with the flow of passengers.

CHAPTER 8

Jasmine

The quaint seaside town was supposed to be Jasmine's escape—a solo weekend getaway meticulously planned to offer respite from the predictability of her marriage to David. Their life together was comfortable, built on years of shared history and quiet affection, but the spontaneous, fiery passion of their early years felt like a distant memory, a faded photograph tucked away in an album. Jasmine had hoped the solitude, and the sound of the ocean would rekindle something within her, a spark that had begun to feel increasingly elusive in their daily lives. She hadn't anticipated the raw, visceral pull of the local fisherman she met at the weathered pier on her first afternoon.

His name was Kai, and he possessed a rugged, untamed energy that was the antithesis of David's gentle, intellectual demeanor. His hands, calloused from hauling in the day's catch, moved with an instinctive grace, and the sun-etched lines around his dark, intense eyes hinted at a life lived on the edge of the wild. When those eyes met Jasmine's as he offered her a sample of his smoked fish, the polite transaction felt charged with an undercurrent of something far more potent. A forbidden heat flared instantly within her, a stark contrast to the quiet contentment she was supposed to be seeking.

That evening, in an attempt to shake off the lingering awkwardness of dining alone, Jasmine found herself at a small seaside tavern where the local wine flowed a little too freely. The salty air and the tranquil crash of waves outside seemed to amplify the restless yearning within her. When Kai, who was nursing a beer at the bar, caught her eye and offered to show her a hidden cove "where the stars put on a better show," the invitation felt less about celestial navigation and more about a core, unspoken need that mirrored her own.

He led her away from the tavern's glow, along a narrow, winding path that hugged the coastline. The air grew crisper, carrying the sharp tang of salt and brine. Above them the night sky was a breathtaking tapestry, a velvet expanse ablaze with a million piercing stars, each one glittering like a diamond. The path descended, growing steeper, until the roar of the ocean intensified, a deep, boisterous thunder. Rounding a final bend, they stepped into a small, almost magical alcove barely visible from the path. Here a narrow waterfall cascaded down a sheer rock face, its silvery ribbon shimmering under the starlight, pooling into a clear, shallow basin before trickling out to meet the incoming tide. The soft murmur of the falling water served as an intimate, natural screen, making them feel utterly alone, completely cut off from the world.

In the darkness, against the hypnotic crashing of the waves, the melodic trickle of the waterfall, and the warm pulse of the wine in her veins, Jasmine's desire erupted with a fierce, reckless abandon. The image of David's familiar, predictable touch vanished, replaced by an insistent craving for Kai's rough hands on her body. She needed the scrape of his calloused fingers against her bare skin, the engulfing grip that would leave no doubt about his raw intent. She needed the taste of salt and untamed masculinity on his lips as he devoured her mouth. She could feel the urgency of their touch, their haste as they tore away each other's clothes fueled. The cool, damp sand pressed against her naked back, the rough wool of his fisherman's sweater scratching against her thighs as he pinned her beneath him, the weight of his hard body a thrilling transgression—every sensation heightened, carnal, and intensely forbidden. The comfortable boundaries of her marriage dissolved in a cocktail of alcohol and desire, replaced by the magnetic pull of this stranger.

Kai's hand found hers in the darkness, his grip tightening around her fingers with an intense heat that mirrored the inferno raging within her. The secluded cove had become a stage for the raw, uninhibited encounter her body was scream- ing for, a dangerous deviation from the quiet solitude she had intended to seek. The stars above seemed to mock the vows she'd made, and the only constellation Jasmine truly saw was the burning desire reflected in Kai's eyes.

He pulled her closer, his mouth descending to claim hers in a brutal, hungry kiss that tasted of wine, salt, and immediate possession. His tongue plunged, mimicking the invasion her body craved, sending a current of fire straight to her core. Her hands clawed at his broad back, impatient to feel more of him, to fuse their bodies together. He responded with a growl, his large, capable hands fumbling with the buttons of her dress, tearing them off in his haste. The cool night air was a shock against her exposed skin. Quickly replaced by the scorching heat of his hands as they found her breasts. Molding them, his thumbs circling her sensitive nipples until they stood erect, taut and demanding.

A moan escaped her as he pushed her gently against the damp sand, the gritty texture, a contrast to the burning heat of his lips as they trailed down her neck, across her collarbone, into the valley between her breasts. She arched her back, offering herself, wordlessly pleading for more. His fingers, strong and sure, moved with agonizing slowness, pushing her skirt up, brushing past her thighs, then expertly sliding beneath the soft silk of her panties. His touch, illicit and erotic, sent electric surges through her, a direct conduit to the core of her femininity.

His thumb found her, pressing, rubbing, teasing with exquisite precision. Her hips began an automatic bucking, a wild swaying against his hand, silently pleading for release. The friction built, a teasing, tormenting pressure, driving her higher and higher. Her vision blurred, her ears filling with the roar of the ocean and the rush of the waterfall as his expert fingers coaxed her closer and closer to that ultimate, explosive release. The quakes started deep inside, building, building, promising to tear her senses apart, but the final, rending climax remained tantalizingly, piercingly out of reach.

Then, still working its magic between her legs, his hand shifted. His other hand found her own, guiding it to the hard, straining bulge beneath his jeans. Her fingers wrapped around him, feeling the throbbing, pulsing heat, the undeniable proof of his arousal, a perfect match for her own. He let out a low groan, leaning in close, his breath hot against her ear as his hips began a slow, deliberate grind against her hand, mirroring the motion of his fingers inside her. She could feel the tip of him pressing against the wet silk of her panties, a blunt, insistent demand. Every brush, every rub, every subtle shift of their bodies together in the dark cove pushed her closer to the brink of abandon, her body crying out for a culmination that felt impossibly close, yet forever withheld.

A sudden, sharp beam of light cut through the darkness, sweeping across the beach. Jasmine blinked, her breath catching, a gasp escaping her lips. The world snapped back into focus with a disorienting lurch. She was standing on the secluded path, her hand still hovering near the invitation to the hidden cove, the night air crisp against her skin. Kai was right beside her, his hand still gently holding hers, his eyes just as dark but glinting with polite inquiry, not the insatiable drive of moments ago.

"Everything all right?" he asked, his voice a casual rumble, completely devoid of the throaty rasp that had commanded her body.

The heat that had consumed her vanished, replaced by a sudden chill. The scent of him, the feel of his body, the residual warmth of his hand evaporated. She shivered. An unquenchable longing lingered, a constant, low-level hum that resonated with the silence of the night. The beam of light passed, leaving them once again in the dim privacy of the path, but the magic was irrevocably broken. It had all been in her head. Each magnetic stare, each subtle contact, every kiss, every illicit brush of fingers, every coaxing caress that had brought her to the crest of the wave—it had all been a waking dream, a performance with a cast of one.

With a tremor of uncertainty, she dropped his hand.

CHAPTER 9

Sarah

The garishly lit gymnasium, decorated with wilted streamers and suffused with the faint scent of stale pizza, was intended to prompt a nostalgic trip down memory lane for all the former classmates who gathered there. For Sarah, however, it was a minefield of awkward smiles and forced small talk. Her carefully constructed adult life felt miles away from the insecurities and unrequited crushes of her teenage years.

Then he walked in.

Jake "Razor" Riley. Even his nickname sent a charge of rebellious energy through Sarah, a reminder of the raw, untamed desire he'd ignited in her young heart. He was older now, the rough edges softened slightly, but the smoldering intensity in his eyes remained, hinting that the trouble he used to cause was far from over.

Their eyes met across the crowded room, and a spark of recognition—and something far more potent—flared between them. The years melted away, and Sarah was once again the shy girl secretly yearning for the attention of the school's notorious bad boy.

As they caught up, a charged undercurrent of unspoken memories and simmering attraction laced their conversation. Their shared history ignited a yearning in Sarah that was both thrilling and terrifying in its intensity.

In the confines of her thoughts, the gymnasium dissolved into a dimly lit motel room, the air thick with the scent of cigarettes and forbidden desire. The rest of her awkward former classmates vanished as she conjured an intimate space where her teenage fantasies could finally become real.

This was her chance to rewrite the past. She felt Jake's hands, those hands that used to grip the handlebars of his motorcycle with such expert control, now exploring the curves of her body with a lust that mirrored the longing she'd suppressed for years.

She felt the urgency of his touch as they tore away each other's clothes. A cheap motel bed materialized, becoming a stage for their forbidden encounter, the sounds of their passion a stark contrast to the polite chatter of the reunion . . .

The boundaries of her adult life shattered as Jake's hand brushed her own beneath the harsh gym lights. His fingers tangled with hers in a steadfast grip that sent ripples of sensation rushing through her, the years of restraint and polite distance crumbling.

"Remember room 203?" Jake's voice was low, intimate. "Always empty. Always . . . interesting possibilities."

Sarah's breath hitched. The memory of that room, the unspoken dares and stolen glances, ignited a fire within her that threatened to consume her. The reunion once more faded into the background, replaced by the gut-turning anticipation of finally claiming the desires that had haunted her since adolescence.

"Meet me there," Jake murmured, his gaze burning into hers. "Ten minutes."

Her heart hammered against her ribs as she slipped away from the crowded gymnasium, a thrill of reckless abandon coursing through her veins. The familiar scent of floor wax and aging textbooks in the deserted hallway of the high school stirred a potent mix of nostalgia and illicit excitement. Room 203 was exactly as she remembered—dusty lab tables, faded anatomical charts, an aura of forgotten experiments.

Jake was already there, leaning against a lab table, his eyes dark and unwavering as they locked on to hers. The years melted away, and they were teenagers again.

Without a word, he reached for her, his hands gripping her hips, pulling her close until her body collided with his hard frame. His kiss was raw and urgent, a claim that seemed to match the years of unacknowledged desire. Sarah's hands found their way to his hair, her fingers tangling in its familiar roughness.

They shed their clothes with a flustered urgency, the sounds of zippers and rustling fabric echoing in the quiet room. The cool surface of the lab table became their makeshift bed as Jake's body covered hers, the hard wood a stark contrast to the raw heat building between them. His mouth devoured hers, his tongue plunging deep, as if to make up for lost time.

His hands roamed her body with ardent longing, cupping her breasts, his thumbs teasing her nipples until they hardened beneath his touch. Sarah arched against him, her own hands exploring the solid muscles of his back, the familiar contours she had only dared imagine as a teenager.

Their breath came in hurried, broken bursts, and the harmonic slap of skin against skin filled the vacant classroom, a forbidden symphony echoing through the empty halls of their shared past. The thrill of being in that space, the risk of discovery, only amplified the raw, uninhibited passion of their encounter. The years of polite distance had shattered, replaced by a visceral, long-awaited eruption of teenage hormones finally unleashed.

Jake's fingers trailed lower, pushing past the waistband of her skirt, then decisively sliding under the hem, his touch burning a fiery path along her inner thigh. He found the delicate silk of her panties and without hesitation slipped a finger beneath the lace, seeking, finding, then skillfully stroking the sensitive skin there. Sarah gasped against his mouth, her hips beginning an instinctive sway, a wordless supplication for more. The friction built, a dizzying, driving pressure, pushing her higher and higher. His other hand found her breast, kneading it firmly, his fingers expertly circling her nipple, drawing a raw moan from her throat.

He broke the kiss, his lips trailing hot, wet promises down her neck, across her collarbone, pausing at the sweet spot of her neck. His gaze, dark and determined, locked on to hers as his hips began a slow, deliberate grind against her, the thick, unyielding length of him a blunt, insistent demand against her lower belly. He shifted his hand, leaving her briefly, then returning, guiding himself inside her with a slow, deliberate thrust that nearly sent her over the edge. The world narrowed to just the sensation of him filling her, the exquisite friction, the shared dance that threatened to propel her into a mind-numbing culmination. Every nerve ending hummed, every muscle clenched, her body a taut bowstring, drawn to its limit, ready for release.

A harsh, grating sound cut through the haze. A piercing, metallic screech echoed through the room, followed by the shattering of glass.

The fluorescent lights flickered, buzzing back to life with a jarring intensity. Sarah blinked, her eyes snapping open, a sharp, disorienting chill washing over her. She was standing in the middle of the crowded gymnasium, her heart hammering, her body still humming with unmet desire. Jake was several feet away, his expression neutral, puzzled, looking toward the source of the crash—a broken window in the far corner where a rogue basketball had clearly done its work. He was holding a fallen stack of yearbooks, the sound of the crash still reverberating in the sudden silence.

The heat that had consumed her vanished, replaced by the faint, stale air of the school. The scent of him, the feel of his body, the imagined pressure of his fingertips—all of it dispersed, leaving her with the embarrassing reality of her own tense, panting rhythm. Her body still pulsed with the echo of denial, the magic irrevocably broken. Every heated gaze, every kiss, every illicit brush of fingers, every coaxing caress that had brought her to the very moment she would break—it had all been in her head. A tremor ran through her. She smoothed down her clothes as a chilling emptiness settled in, more disturbing than the stale pizza and wilted streamers of the reunion.

CHAPTER 10

Eleanor

The fluorescent lights of the Mega Mart hummed dully, a soundtrack to Eleanor's Tuesday afternoon. Her cart, a metallic extension of her weary arms, bumped along the crowded aisles, navigating the slow dance of other shoppers equally intent on their lists and avoiding eye contact. At forty-eight, Eleanor often felt like she'd become a ghost in these spaces, a familiar fixture that no one truly saw. She was the woman reaching for the low-fat yogurt, the one comparing prices of canned tomatoes, the one patiently waiting her turn at the deli counter—a cog in the consumer machine, unremarkable and unseen.

Today, the feeling was a little heavier than usual. Michael, her husband of twenty-five years, had been preoccupied lately, his attention often drifting toward the television or his latest woodworking project. Their conversations felt functional, a check-in regarding daily needs rather than sharing inner thoughts. Sometimes, amid the simplicity of their life, a subtle pang would settle in her chest, bringing her face-to-face with her own invisibility.

She rounded the corner into the canned goods aisle, her eyes scanning the shelves for diced peaches. A younger man, maybe in his early thirties, was reaching for a can on the shelf just above where she was looking. He was dressed casually in a worn band T-shirt and jeans, his brow furrowed in concentration as he read the label.

Their hands brushed, a fleeting, accidental touch, the kind that usually prompted a mumbled "Sorry" and a quick withdrawal. But this was different. Their eyes met. His was a surprising shade of brown, crinkling slightly at the corners as a genuine, unhurried smile spread across his face. It wasn't a flirtatious smile or a polite, obligatory one; it was a smile that seemed to acknowledge her presence, a brief spark of human connection in the sterile environment of the supermarket. His gaze held hers for a beat longer than necessary, a wordless hello.

A small tremor went through her body. He finally took his can of beans, and as he turned, this time it was his shoulder that brushed hers, a more deliberate contact that lingered for a moment. He offered another soft smile, a warmth in his eyes that felt impossibly intimate, before he moved on. Eleanor's pulse quickened.

A few minutes later, as she debated which brand of coffee to buy, she glanced up to find him at the other end of the aisle, looking at bottled water. His gaze, dark and intense, found hers again, holding steady. This time the simmering intensity she saw there felt like a challenge, a question. He didn't look away until Eleanor flustered, ducked her head, her cheeks warm.

Then, at the deli counter, she felt his presence behind her. The scent of him—clean, subtly masculine—reached her nostrils. She could feel his eyes on her back. When her number was called, she turned to find him directly behind her in line, a faint smirk playing on his lips as he met her gaze. This was no longer accidental. This was a covert pursuit, an unspoken acknowledgment of the crackling tension between them.

The fantasy surged, consuming her. The mundane surroundings of the Mega Mart dissolved, replaced by a charged, almost predatory anticipation.

She wheeled her cart toward the checkout, her heart hammering with a pulse that had nothing to do with her age or her grocery list. She spotted an open lane, and as if guided by an invisible string, he chose the lane right next to hers. They loaded their groceries onto separate conveyor belts, but the space between the lanes felt nonexistent. Their shoulders brushed as they both reached for their wallets, a deliberate graze that sent a wave of illicit thoughts through her. The cashier's small talk faded to a background hum as Eleanor's focus narrowed to the man beside her. His arm, corded with muscle, brushed hers as he reached for his wallet. His scent, a potent blend of musk and something uniquely masculine, once more filled her nostrils. He glanced at her, his eyes molten brown, and a slow, knowing smile spread across his face, sending shivers down her spine.

"Looks like we're on the same wavelength today," he murmured, his voice a low, gravelly rumble that vibrated through her.

Eleanor just managed a breathless laugh; her own voice caught in her throat.

As they paid, the fantasy intensified. This wasn't just a simple acknowledgment anymore. This was a powerful, unspoken invitation.

Outside in the parking lot, the asphalt shimmered under the afternoon sun. Eleanor fumbled with her keys at the trunk of her car. She was wearing a comfortable, flowy sundress today, the soft fabric doing little to hide the sudden quickening of her breath. She heard his voice beside her.

"Need a hand with those, ma'am?"

His car was parked just two spaces down from hers, a sleek, dark muscle car that looked utterly out of place beside her sensible sedan. It wasn't coincidence; it was fate, or rather, the blueprint drawn by her untamed desire.

Before she could answer, he was at her trunk, effortlessly lifting bags and placing them inside. His proximity was intoxicating, the brush of his arm against hers as he reached past her sending a wave of heat through her.

"Thanks," she managed, her voice huskier than she intended.

He straightened, his gaze lingering on her, dark and intense. "You know," he said, his voice dropping, "I'm making dinner tonight. Nothing fancy, just . . . a good meal. And I have a feeling you'd be excellent company." His eyes held hers, a question in their depths. "What do you say, Eleanor? Want to ditch the leftovers and join me instead?"

Her breath hitched. This was it, the forbidden offer. "I . . ." she started, her inner world racing, discarding every sensible thought.

He pulled a pen from his pocket, scribbled something on a receipt, and pressed it into her hand. His fingers brushed hers again, lingering for a beat, sending a shock wave through her. "My number. Text me your address, and I'll send mine. Dinners at eight." His thumb stroked the back of her hand lightly before he let go.

Eleanor watched him walk to his car, every movement radiating confidence and a dangerous allure. She clutched the receipt, the numbers blurring, her heart pounding a jittery drum against her ribs.

At eight o'clock, she found herself pulling up to his small, unassuming house, the porch light glowing like a beacon.

He opened the door before she even knocked, and the moment their eyes met, the pretense of dinner shattered. The scent of his home was a primal, woodsy musk—an aroma not of food but of him, of uninhibited masculinity, of a profound urge that mirrored her own. His gaze stripped away her sensible clothing, her years, her inhibitions, leaving her exposed and craving. The soft glow of the living room lamps cast long shadows, blurring the lines of reality and desire.

He didn't speak. He simply stepped back, letting her cross the abyss, and then closed the door behind her with a soft click that resonated like the finality of a choice. His eyes burned into hers, and then, slowly, deliberately, his gaze dropped to her mouth, then lowered, to her breasts, her hips, before returning to her eyes. The air crackled with silent tension.

"The only thing being eaten tonight," he murmured, his voice a low, husky growl, "is you, Eleanor."

His mouth was on hers before the words fully left his lips, a savage claim that left her reeling. He wasted no time, his hands gripping her waist, lifting her effortlessly, never breaking the searing kiss. Her legs instinctively wrapped around his hips, her sundress riding high on her thighs. He carried her like that, her body plastered against his, his mouth devouring hers, until he reached a large, rustic dining table in the center of the room. With a heavy grunt, he gently laid her on her back on the cool boards.

Her breathing hitched, her vision swimming with desire as he loomed over her, his eyes burning into hers. He moved quickly, efficiently, spreading her legs wide, his hands sliding under the soft fabric of her sundress. With a single, firm pull, he yanked her panties to the side, exposing her fully. His gaze devoured her, a raw, hungry assessment that sent a shiver of intense anticipation through her. Then, without warning, he lowered his head, burying his face into her innermost parts, his hot mouth and teasing tongue immediately finding her pulsating clitoris.

Eleanor let out a strangled whimper, a raw, untamed sound, her fingers tangling in his hair, pulling him closer, fighting for more. The world narrowed to the exquisite torture of his mouth, his tongue, his fingers as they worked her mercilessly, driving her higher than she'd ever been. His lips suckled, his tongue flicked and swirled, and his fingers probed deeper, finding and teasing her most sensitive folds. Her body arched against the hard table, her hips bucking in an instinctive dance, mutely begging for the release he was building yet so exquisitely denying. Every nerve ending screamed, every muscle clenched; she was a breath from the pinnacle of sensation. She could feel the taut, ruthless strength of him pressing against her inner thigh, a silent, pulsing promise of what was yet to come, driving her further to the edge. The waves of sensation inside her began to seize, suspending her at the apex of elation, moments from falling, threatening to detonate her senses. She was poised, trembling on the verge of total surrender . . .

Then, with a sudden, decisive movement, he pulled his head away, leaving her gasping, pleading, undone. He wasted no time. With a low growl, he hauled her off the table, and before her feet could fully touch the ground, he bent her over the sturdy wood, pushing her hips forward, her sundress riding high on her back. Her hands instinctively braced on the table, knuckles white. He was right behind her, his hard body pressing into hers, and she felt the unmistakable, blunt prod of his erection against her. With a fierce, intense thrust, he took her from behind, filling her with a force that stole her breath and sent a shock wave through her core. The friction was immediate, demanding, driving her back, back, back against him. He began to move, a savage, barbaric plunge that pushed her body to the snapping point of her composure, each thrust bringing her closer to the agonizing climax she craved. Her nails dug into the wood; her teeth bit into her lip as the pressure built, relentlessly, unbearably—

A sudden beep echoed through the silent air.

Eleanor blinked, her eyes snapping open. She was standing in the busy Mega Mart checkout line, her cart piled high with groceries. The cashier, a young girl with bored eyes, was scanning her items, a low, electronic beep accompanying each swipe. The man—that younger man from the canned goods aisle—was nowhere in sight.

The scent of cleaning products and freshly baked bread replaced the intoxicating musk of desire, accompanied by the sounds of crying babies and overly cheerful music. The spectral caresses of his mouth, the excruciatingly close promise of release—the entire scene, every touch, every word—had been a figment of her imagination.

The crumpled receipt was still in her hand, but it was just her grocery list, not a phone number. Haltingly and with visible effort, she pushed her cart forward as the cashier finished scanning, the abrupt freeze of reality sharper than the refrigerated air in the aisle she'd just left. Eleanor was just a ghost haunting the Mega Mart, unseen, untouched, and hollow.

CHAPTER 11

Olivia

The sterile confines of Olivia's hotel room felt like a cage. The business trip, meant to be a professional triumph, had devolved into a lonely routine of meetings and soulless dinners. A restless energy reverberated beneath her composure, a yearning for something more than the calculated interactions of the corporate world.

Then she met him at the hotel bar.

His name was Forrest, and he possessed a laid-back charm that starkly contrasted with the stiff suits and power plays of her colleagues. His eyes, a warm hazel, held a playful glint that hinted at a life lived outside the boardroom, and his smile sent a shiver of unexpected excitement through her.

Their conversation flowed effortlessly, evincing a shared appreciation for good wine and a mutual weariness of the corporate grind. But beneath the surface, a potent current of attraction crackled, a silent acknowledgment of a shared longing for something more than polite discourse.

As the evening deepened, fueled by wine and the anonymity of being away from home, Olivia's imagination took flight. The impersonal hotel bar became a dimly lit, intimate lounge, the other patrons fading to a blurry backdrop for a forbidden encounter. The gleaming facade of her professional life dissolved, replaced by the raw, uninhibited desires she usually kept carefully concealed.

A burning need for indulgence eclipsed her inner world. She pictured Forrest's hands, those hands that held his wineglass with such casual grace, exploring the curves of her body with a thirst that mirrored her own. The prospect of giving herself to a stranger in a strange city elicited almost dangerous excitement. The thrill of being discovered, the lack of consequences, only amplified the intensity.

The boundaries of her carefully constructed life blurred and shattered in the heat of her fantasy. She pictured the stolen moments, the raw physicality, the complete surrender to a desire that was both a rebellion and an escape. The charming stranger had become the catalyst for a dream that unleashed the wilder, more uninhibited woman she'd always kept hidden.

Forrest's hand brushed hers across the table. "My room?" His voice was a low, husky invitation, his eyes locking on Olivia's.

A spark of reckless abandon ignited within her. The constraints of her marriage, the carefully constructed walls of her professional life seemed to melt away in the face of this immediate, undeniable connection. "Yours," she breathed, the single word a surrender to temptation.

The elevator ride to Forrest's floor was charged with tension, the silence punctuated only by the pleasant hum of the machinery. Their eyes never left each other, a wordless communication of escalating desire passing between them.

The moment the door to Forrest's hotel room closed behind them, the pretense of polite conversation vanished. He reached for Olivia, his hands gripping her hips with a possessive ardor. His kiss was immediate, demanding, a raw claim that mirrored the unspoken desires of the entire evening. Olivia met his passion with equal fervor, her hands tangling in his hair, pulling him closer. Their clothes, shed with fevered urgency, landed in heaps on the carpet. The king-sized bed became their immediate destination, a stage for uncorking the current that had been simmering beneath the surface all night.

Forrest's mouth blazed a trail down Olivia's neck, his lips and teeth leaving a searing imprint. His hands roamed her body, cupping her breasts, his thumbs teasing her nipples until they were hard beneath his touch. Olivia arched against him, her own hands exploring the solid contours of his body, the feel of his bare skin igniting a primal response. His breath, hot and wine laced, fanned across her flushed skin, every inhale intoxicating and dizzying her.

He tore his mouth from hers only to whisper urgent promises against her ear, promises of sweetness and complete abandon, before trailing his tongue lower, across her collarbone, down to the valley between her breasts. His teeth gently nipped at her sternum, sending shivers through her as his hands continued their fervent exploration, tracing the curve of her waist, pushing past the lace of her panties. His fingers found her already slick and warm, and he began to stroke her with a dexterity that was both tender and relentlessly demanding.

Olivia gasped, her back arching further as Forrest's fingers worked their magic, pressing, circling, teasing, pulling her deeper into the swirling vortex of sensation. Her nails dug into the plush comforter beneath them as the rush intensified, building rapidly. He moved his mouth lower, following his hands, his hot breath ghosting over her sensitive skin before his tongue flicked out, tasting her, consuming her. He devoted himself to her, his mouth a skilled instrument, suckling, teasing, drawing out soft moans from her throat that she barely recognized as her own.

Her hips began a primal grind against his face, speechlessly entreating him for the release he was so exquisitely building yet denying. The air grew thick with the scent of their combined desire, a musky sweetness that clouded her senses. The world outside the hotel room faded, replaced by the pounding of her own blood in her ears, the ragged sound of their breathing, and the delicious, unbearable friction he was creating.

He shifted, rising slightly, his eyes burning into hers, filled with raw need. His body pressed against her, the hard length of him a throbbing presence against her inner thigh. He lowered himself, aligning their bodies perfectly, and with a slow, deliberate thrust, he entered her, filling her with a profound, stretching completeness that stole her breath. Olivia gave a muffled gasp, her body clenching around him. The friction was immediate, demanding, driving her back against the mattress.

Forrest began to move, plunging into her again and again, driving her to the edge of her physical endurance, each thrust bringing her closer to the agonizing climax she craved. Her legs wrapped tighter around his waist, pulling him deeper, demanding more. He leaned in, his lips brushing her ear, whispering guttural urgings that only fueled her raw yearning for him. The sounds of their bodies meeting, their slick, sweat-filled movements, filled the room, amplifying the illicit thrill of their encounter. The intensity built, a spiraling crescendo of heat and pressure, every one of Olivia's nerve endings screaming as the build-up of sensation threatened to consume her. She was a coiled spring, wound to its limit, moments from snapping. Her entire being trembled with longing for release. She gripped him, her body rigid, on the summit of obliteration . . .

A sudden, jarring knock echoed through the silent hotel room.

Olivia's eyes snapped open, a sharp, disorienting chill washing over her. She was lying in the middle of her own sterile hotel bed. The crisp white sheets tangled around her. Forrest was nowhere in sight.

The scent of stale air-conditioning replaced the intoxicating musk of desire; the dull hum of the mini fridge replaced the heavy breathing and intimate sounds that had filled her senses moments before. The faint echo of his touch, his mouth, the excruciatingly close promise of release, it was all only a carefully crafted vision, a private fabrication, existing only in her own reality.

Another knock came, louder this time, followed by a muffled "Housekeeping!" from outside the door. Raw, unfulfilled need burned within her. She pulled the sheets tighter around her as emptiness filled her gut, colder than the air-conditioned room.

CHAPTER 12

Isabelle

T he air in the cabin hummed with the easy laughter of Isabelle's girlfriends, the scent of popcorn, and the gentle clink of wineglasses. Isabelle, however, felt a restless energy stirring beneath her relaxed exterior. This girls' trip to Broken Bow, Oklahoma, was supposed to be a carefree escape, a weekend of camaraderie and shared jokes. But beneath the surface she felt a subtle yearning, a longing for something that wasn't on the itinerary.

Earlier that afternoon, a minor issue with the cabin's Wi-Fi had sent her to the main office, and that was where she'd met Liam. He was the property manager, a man whose easy charm and worn jeans seemed at home against the beautiful backdrop of the Ouachita Mountains—a far cry from the refined professionalism she usually encountered. His eyes, a startling shade of deep blue, held a knowing warmth that sent a shiver of unexpected interest through her. He fixed the Wi-Fi quickly, but their conversation lingered, a natural ease forming between them. She learned he lived in one of the smaller, secluded cabins on the property. As she left, his parting smile felt like a quiet invitation.

Now, as her friends finally succumbed to the wine and drifted off to sleep, a reckless decision solidified in Isabelle's mind. The soft glow of her phone screen illuminated a text message: *Trouble sleeping? Hot tub's perfect under the stars.*

It was from Liam.

She slipped out of the cabin, the crisp night air a stark contrast to the heat already building inside her.

The path to Liam's cabin was dimly lit by scattered string lights, and the distant sound of crickets filled the night. His cabin was tucked away, private, the low hum of a hot tub audible even before she reached the porch. He opened the door before she could knock, his eyes immediately locking with hers.

"Figured you'd come," Liam murmured, his voice a low, husky rumble that seemed to reverberate through her bones. He stepped aside, letting her pass into the dimly lit, cozy cabin. The air was thick with the scent of pine and something else—something uniquely masculine and intensely inviting.

There was no small talk, no hesitation. Their eyes held, a wordless understanding passing between them. Then he simply reached for her, his hands finding her waist, pulling her flush against his hard frame. His kiss was immediate, demanding, a raw claim that stripped away every last inhibition. Isabelle met his passion with equal ferocity, her hands tangling in his dark hair, pulling him closer, grasping for connection.

Their clothes, frantically torn off, landed haphazardly all over the cabin's rustic furniture. They stumbled toward the back door and then into the steaming hot tub, the warm, bubbling water instantly enveloping them. The contrast between the cool night air on Isabelle's face and the scorching heat of the water, coupled with Liam's insistent body pressed against hers, electrified her senses.

In the swirling currents, he pulled her onto his lap, her legs wrapping around his waist, her core pressing against his hard erection. His mouth devoured hers, a deep, consuming kiss that left her breathless, tasting of the wine they'd shared and the heady intoxication that now consumed her. His hands roamed, slick with water, across her skin, cupping her breasts, his thumbs circling her nipples until they hardened into peaks, straining for more.

He broke the kiss, his lips trailing a searing path down her neck, along her shoulder, across the delicate curve of her collarbone. The hot water churned around them, the bubbles massaging her skin, intensifying every touch. His hands slid lower, finding the heat between her thighs. He pushed gently, coaxing her legs wider, and his fingers, strong and deliberate, began to part her.

Isabelle gasped, her body arching into his touch as his thumb found her clitoris, pressing, circling, then dipping, sliding. He found the pulsing core of her and began to work it with a relentless, expert coaxing that stole her breath and sent internal quakes rocketing through her. She clutched at his shoulders, her fingers digging into his wet skin as her pleasure escalated, an unbearable, driving current that threatened to overwhelm her. The water surged around them, but the only sound she registered was her own short, ragged breaths. He brought his mouth down, his hot breath ghosting over her most sensitive flesh, before his tongue flicked out, rasping her, teasing her, devouring her with an intensity that made her writhe against him.

"So wet for me, Isabelle," he rasped against her, his voice a low, guttural growl. He lifted her slightly, adjusting their positions in the swirling water, his erection pressing against her entrance. He teased her, rubbing the thick, throbbing head against her slick folds, letting her feel the immense pressure, the promise of ultimate satisfaction, before pulling back just an inch.

Her hips bucked, her body's mute appeal for him to finally claim her. He responded by grinding against her, the tension mounting, fueling the urge within her yet withholding the climax her body craved. The hot water churned around them, carrying the scent of their mingled arousal. She could feel the taut, insistent presence of his erection against her inner thigh, driving her further to the edge. The muscles deep within her clenched, her body poised on the brink, her senses about to explode in a blinding, roaring wave. She was there, right there, trembling, about to break . . .

Then, with a sudden, forceful shift, he pulled her out of the hot tub, the cold night air hitting her skin like a shock, leaving her gasping. He didn't let go; instead, he hauled her roughly against the side of the cabin, the rough-hewn logs digging into her back. Her legs were still wrapped around his waist, her wet body plastered against his, the hot tub's steam rising around them like mist.

"Not yet," he growled, his voice tight with restraint. He twisted her, bending her over the hot tub's edge, her chest pressed against the cool, hard rim, her legs dangling, still wrapped around him. He hiked her higher, her exposed bottom glistening in the moonlight, and with a grunt of raw anticipation, he plunged into her from behind, filling her with a force that stole her breath and sent a shock wave through her core. The friction was immediate, demanding, the searing heat consuming her. As Liam began to move, his deep, urgent thrusting rocked her entire world, driving her body back against him with each powerful plunge. He drove into her relentlessly, his hands gripping her hips, his thrusts deepening, forcing her higher, faster, further than she had ever been. Her nails dug into the wooden railing of the hot tub, her head thrown back, her teeth biting into her lip as the pressure built, relentlessly, unbearably, threatening to rip her apart. She hung suspended, ready to fall into the abyss—

A sudden splash erupted beside her. Isabelle's eyes snapped open, a sharp, disorienting chill washing over her. She was lying in the hot tub outside the cabin she shared with her girlfriends, the warm, bubbling water swirling around her. Her phone, which she must have set on the edge, had slipped into the water, its screen now dark. Liam was nowhere in sight. The warmth, the immediacy, the unbidden connection . . . all of it had melted away.

The scent of chlorine and pine needles replaced the intoxicating musk of desire. The heavy breathing and sensual moans that had filled her senses moments before gave way to the gentle gurgle of the jets.

One of her friends, stirring from the cabin, called out sleepily, "Isabelle? You okay out there? Heard a splash!"

A restless murmur of desire lingered, leaving behind a hollow torment. With a weak, trembling hand, she pulled herself out of the hot tub, the glow of fantasy evaporating, a sudden chill overtaking her, more biting than the cool night air.

BONUS CHAPTER 13

Joanna

Now that she was nearing fifty, Joanna often found her professional life as the manager of the Botanical Gardens a source of stability. Her days were a whirlwind as she juggled the demands of her career along with the relentless energy of her two active young children. Between soccer practices, school events, and the endless stream of questions and requests that come with raising young kids, Joanna's life outside of work was a vibrant, if exhausting, tapestry of activity that almost made up for the desolation of her sexless marriage.

To break up the routine at the Gardens, Joanna often found camaraderie and easy banter with her "work hubby," Luke. Theirs was a comfortable, platonic affection, and he had become something of a daily support system for her. Yet, recently, one figure had begun to subtly shift her internal landscape: Harrison, a Gardens employee who reported directly to her. He stirred a different kind of longing, an illicit yearning, a craving for the taboo.

Harrison was a bright, capable young man, and she'd hired him after recognizing his friendly nature and learning he was looking for extra income. Knowing the Masonic Lodge where she was a member often hired part-time help, she'd used her connections to help him secure a bartending position there. This added another layer to the forbidden thrill—the manager-employee dynamic now intertwined with the member-bartender allure.

Joanna found herself drawn to the Lodge lounge four or five nights a week, conveniently timed with Harrison's shifts. After spending eight hours a day working alongside him at the Gardens, where she held authority, she'd often seek out the dim ambience of the bar, where he held a different kind of sway. She vividly remembered the subtle thrill that had coursed through her in the early days of Harrison working at the Lodge. Several of the female members, their eyes clearly appreciative, had approached her directly, their inquiries laced with curiosity: "Joanna, where did you find him?" "Where did he come from?" She'd felt a distinct sense of pride in knowing she was the one who had brought this undeniably attractive man into their shared space. This subtle sense of ownership, coupled with the exhaustion of her daily life and the yearning for a different kind of connection, had planted a small seed of interest within her.

Harrison was dedicated to his fitness, his toned physique evident even beneath his Gardens uniform and certainly on display in the more relaxed setting of the Masonic Lodge. And yes, Joanna had fleetingly registered the way his comfortable sweatpants sometimes . . . emphasized certain aspects of his anatomy, a detail she'd immediately tried to dismiss as unprofessional observation, though it still occasionally flickered at the edges of her awareness. The fact that she had begun to seek him out in a different setting, night after night, spoke volumes about the small, insistent seed of something akin to a crush that had taken root within her—a forbidden allure heightened by their different roles in her life.

The end of the workday one evening cast long shadows across the Botanical Gardens. Joanna, the manager, had just exchanged her usual lighthearted farewell with Luke, their easy familiarity a stark contrast to the nervous anticipation that now fluttered within her as she thought of Harrison. She was tidying her desk, the soft melodies in her earbuds a gentle accompaniment to the hushed calm of the emptying office, when a soft knock echoed on her open door. Joanna instinctively reached up and removed her right earbud, acknowledging the presence in her doorway.

It was Harrison, her employee, his worn duffel bag slung over his shoulder. He lingered in the doorway, a slight hesitation in his posture.

"Bye, Joanna," he said, his voice a little softer than usual.

She looked up, her gaze immediately catching his. There was weariness around his eyes she hadn't noticed earlier. "Harrison, are you okay?" she asked, the concern in her voice holding a warmth that went beyond their professional dynamic.

He offered a small, almost strained smile. "Yeah, just a long day."

But Joanna sensed more. "Is everything all right?" she pressed gently, her gaze unwavering.

He hesitated for another moment, his eyes flicking around the office before returning to hers. "Yeah . . . just tired. Long week, you know?"

"I do," Joanna replied softly, a shared understanding passing between them.

A brief silence hung in the air, charged with a subtle undercurrent that felt far more potent than her easygoing interactions with Luke. Joanna found herself holding his gaze a moment longer than necessary, a silent acknowledgment of the taboo connection, and in that protracted moment, the landscape of her psyche ignited.

Suddenly, the quiet office dissolved, replaced by the vibration of her new, shiny SUV idling in the staff parking lot. It was precisely 11:30 a.m. when she met Harrison there, his worn duffel bag now slung casually over his shoulder. He slid into the passenger seat, the sleek, cool leather molding beneath him. She gave him a quick, knowing glance, then shifted into drive, steering away from the main office buildings and turning onto the public road. The Gardens, usually bustling with visitors, quickly faded in the rearview mirror.

She drove with purpose, the silence in the cab thick with unvoiced desire. She pulled into the parking lot of a small, nondescript motel on the edge of town, its sign discreetly tucked away. She killed the engine.

"Room 107," he murmured, his voice a low, rough rasp, handing her a key card he must have acquired earlier. His eyes, dark and direct, held hers. The invitation was clear, undeniable.

Joanna took the card, her fingers trembling slightly. She didn't hesitate as she led the way to the appropriately marked door.

The moment the door closed behind them, the thin walls of the motel room seemed to disappear. The click of the lock sealed them into a private, illicit world. Joanna turned to Harrison, her gaze bold and direct. He didn't speak. She reached for him, her hands finding the hem of his uniform shirt and pulling it free from his trousers. Her mouth found his with a fierce urgency, her tongue plunging in, an instinctive invasion that stripped away every last pretense of professionalism. Harrison responded with ferocity, his hands tangling in her short hair, pulling her closer, his body arching into hers. The tight confines of the small room amplified the intensity of their movements, trapping in the scent of their mingled desire.

She was the one to pull back first, her breath ragged. Her hands moved with swift precision, unbuttoning his shirt, stripping it from his broad shoulders. Then her fingers went to the buckle of his trousers. She pulled his pants free and tossed them carelessly onto the cheap motel carpet. Her underwear, delicate lace against burning skin, was also swiftly torn off and discarded, leaving her completely exposed from the waist down in the dim light of the room. Her gaze devoured him, a raw, hungry assessment as she watched him strip off the rest of his clothes, revealing his powerful, taut body, his erection magnificent and pulsing with undeniable demand.

She led him to the bed, pulling him down onto the worn sheets. She was over him in an instant, pinning him against the mattress. Her mouth found his again. Her hands worked between his thighs, roughly forcing his knees apart, spreading him wide open. The pressure of her body against his, the raw heat of his skin, was overwhelming. Then her own fingers grazed her wet center, a reminder of her still-simmering need, before she shifted, her hips sliding down.

Joanna positioned herself, her gaze fixed on him, a silent promise in her eyes. Her hands reached out, encircling the thick base of his arousal. She lowered her head, taking him into her mouth, the first touch of his heat sending a tingle through her. Her lips closed around him, warm and wet, her tongue immediately engaging in a slow, deliberate dance. She pulled back slightly, then plunged deeper, taking him in with a fierce, hungry intensity, her throat working around him. She rotated her head, expertly using her tongue and lips to explore every inch of his length, drawing a low, guttural moan from his throat.

Harrison's fingers tangled in her hair, not pulling but holding her firmly as he arched his back into her ministrations. His breath hitched, his body trembling beneath her. She continued her ardent devotion, her cheeks hollowing with each powerful draw, her tongue flicking, swirling, pressing against his underside, then gliding along his sensitive tip. The sounds he made, low groans and sharp gasps, fueled her. She could feel the increasing hardness of him against her tongue, the thickness at his base under her hands. He was nearing his rupture point.

Just as the convulsions began to build in him, she pulled back, a mischievous gleam in her eye. She rose, straddling his hips, her slick, waiting entrance hovering just above his throbbing shaft. His eyes, wide with raw need, watched her every move. When he gave a low groan of anticipation, Joanna slowly, deliberately lowered herself. Mind-numbing sensation overtook her as his magnificent length slid into her, filling her completely.

They began to move, a piston-like motion that shook her core, shook the entire bed, shook her world. Her hands gripped his hips as she drove herself against him. The friction was immediate, consuming, and she rode him relentlessly, forcing herself higher, faster, further than she had ever been. She wrapped her legs around his waist, pulling him deeper, desperately trying to absorb every inch of him. Her nails dug into his back, her head thrown back against the flimsy headboard, her teeth biting into her lip as the pressure built, inexorably, unbearably.

The sounds of their bodies colliding, the wet slap of skin, the ragged sounds of their breathing filled the small room, drowning out everything else. She was spiraling, an irrepressible ascent toward a sensation that promised to consume her entirely. Her core began to contract. She was on the precipice, her whole being vibrating with an intolerable pressure, poised to detonate in a silent, all-consuming convulsion.

He pushed into her one last, powerful time, a deep, shuddering thrust that drew a raw cry from his throat. His body went rigid, his muscles straining, his breath coming in ragged gasps as he reached his own zenith, relinquishing himself deep inside her. Joanna felt his powerful contractions, the hot rush of his release.

But as his body shuddered and then relaxed against hers, as his breathing slowly eased, Joanna remained poised on the very edge. The intense heat of his release was in her, around her, but her own body continued to hum with an electrifying, unreleased pressure. Her muscles remained clenched, her breath hitched, the tight knot in her belly throbbing with a profound, unquenched tension. She had been so close, had felt every exquisite step of his journey, yet her own awaited release stubbornly refused to come. Waves of torment surged within her, unsatiated, vibrant and alive. She was left suspended, yearning, aware of the raw, undeniable reality of what had just transpired yet still trapped in limbo.

The image of Harrison's satisfied face, the motel room, the sounds and sensations all snapped back to nothingness as abruptly as they had begun. Joanna blinked, her gaze refocusing on the reality of her office. Harrison was still there, a hesitant figure framed in her doorway, exactly as he had been moments before. The only sounds were the quiet hum of the office and the gentle music from her earbud.

He was still holding his duffel bag, his eyes still carrying that touch of weariness. His clothes were neat, his hair perfectly in place. Her own desk was tidy, her blouse unruffled, her skirt smooth. Nothing had changed.

"Well, Joanna," he repeated, his voice just as soft as before. "Bye."

Joanna felt a flush creep up her neck, a phantom heat blooming across her skin. The vividness of the fantasy left her breathless; the only physical proof of the journey the deep recesses of her consciousness had just taken her on. Heavy, unreleased tension vibrated through her, sharper now that she knew the depths of ecstasy her imagination could conjure and how excruciatingly far from it her reality was.

"Bye, Harrison," she managed, her voice a little more breathless than she intended, a taut, keen knot of longing coiling in her gut. He gave her a small, polite nod and then, with a final, lingering look, turned and walked away, leaving her alone with the echoing silence of her office and the vibrant, throbbing memory of a lunch break that had never happened.

ACKNOWLEDGMENTS

No book is ever created in isolation, and this one is no exception.

To my copyeditor, Rachel Keith, for her attention to detail and for shaping these words into a sharper reflection of my vision.

To Sharman Wilkinson, whose voice brings this story to life in a way that captures not only the words, but the heartbeat behind them.

To the team at 100 Covers, for crafting a design that reflects the soul of this book in a single glance.

To my family and friends, for their patience, encouragement, and constant reminders that passion is worth pursuing.

And finally, to every reader who picks up this book — thank you for trusting me with your time and your imagination. You are the reason these words exist on the page.

ABOUT THE AUTHOR

Darron Thomas is a Navy Veteran and self-published author whose words dive deep into the unseen worlds of desire, transformation, and truth.

Raised in a household of four generations of women—his sister, mother, grandmother, and great-grandmother—he learned the power of listening, observing, and honoring the quiet strength of women. That foundation became the heartbeat of his writing.

His debut novella, Ctrl+Alt=Desire: Where the Mind Finds Its Escape*, is a bold exploration of the spaces between the ordinary and the forbidden. Written with psychological depth and raw honesty, the work gives voice to women who crave to be seen, heard, and fully known.

Darron's life has been shaped by service, resilience, and creativity—qualities he brings to every story he tells. His vision is clear: to create works that not only entertain, but liberate.